The Adventures of Joe Fenek

Written by Graham Bayes

Drawings by Salvina Louise Aquilina

First published in 2013
by
FARAXA
www.faraxapublishing.com
Email: info@faraxapublishing.com

Printed by Best Print, Qrendi, Malta.

ISBN: 978-99957-0-527-5

Contents

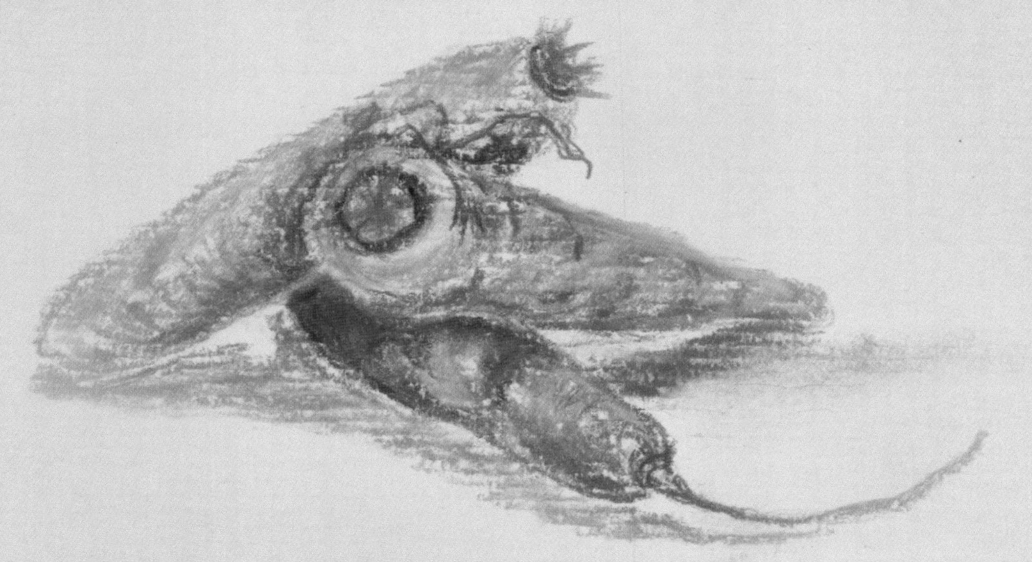

Joe Fenek

Jimmy the rat

Digger the Shrew

Spikey the hedgehog

Tony the rat

Horace the horse

Mario the mouse

Joe Fenek's Lucky escape

Early one morning, two hunters, Manwel and Anton, parked their pick-up truck on the outskirts of the village of Mellieħa, in Malta. They were going to hunt *fenek*, as a rabbit is known in Malta.

They walked towards St Agnes's Tower, also known as the Red Tower, where they knew there were some rabbit warrens. They carried with them their nets and their bagged ferret, and with them walked their dogs.

They used the nets to cover the entrance holes of the warrens and put the bell collars around the neck of the ferret.

Then they released the dog named Sam and the ferret under one of the nets. The ferret raced into the entrance of the warren.

Dozing, deep in the warren, after a having had a midnight feast, Joe suddenly awoke, wondering what the noise could be. He soon realised it was a ferret bell and looking down the tunnel, he saw the ferret running towards him. Joe was so scared that he ran down another tunnel in the warren, which he knew would take him to the base of the big, tree trunk. The ventilation hole was a bit too small for him to get out of, so he had to dig and squeeze his way through.

When Joe got outside, he could see the hunters at the entrance with their nets all spread around, waiting to catch him. He looked around and decided that he needed to run. So that is exactly what he did. He ran and ran and ran.

Trouble was, he got quite tired and had to slow down. Behind him, he could hear something panting and although he was scared, he turned to look. It was Sam whose eyes and teeth were the most frightening thing Joe had ever seen. But he knew he would be in trouble if he kept on running.

So he stopped, put up his paw and said, "Stop. Now before you kill me and before you eat me, can I just say one thing? If you kill me, you will not eat me; the hunter will. So can we come to an agreement? If I pretend I am dead, you could have the chance to eat me later on, when we get back to the farm."

The dog looked at Joe and after some thought agreed. So Joe lay on the ground and pretended to be dead. Sam stood over him and waited for the hunter. When Manwel arrived, he brushed the dog

aside, picked Joe up by the scruff of his neck and threw him into a sack. Manwel walked back to the pick-up truck and threw Joe, in the sack, into the back of the truck. Five minutes later, Anton arrived back at the truck with several sacks, which he also threw into the back of the truck. Sam leapt onto the back of the truck, then Anton and Manwel got back into the truck and proceeded to drive back to the farm. Parked in the driveway was a van.

Manwel took the sack containing Joe and threw it into the back of his van, while Anton took the dog which was barking loudly and the ferret into the outbuildings.

Manwel shouted, "See you," to Anton and started the van up. He drove towards Ċirkewwa where he was going to catch the ferry back to Gozo.

He drove onto the ferry, parked and locked the van, then went up on the deck to watch the sunrise. Meanwhile, Joe was chewing madly at the sack, trying to find a way out. Finally, he managed to get out and was able to look out of the windows of the van. He could hear a lot of noise and see lots of cars, trucks and lorries. He tried really hard to unlock the door, but he was too tired. His legs were weak, he was very dizzy and his tummy

was turning. The boat was going one way, then the other, and Joe was feeling sick.

Suddenly, everything went very quiet and then very noisy, and Joe noticed lots of people getting into the cars. Then he saw Manwel, so he hid himself under the sack and lay very still.

Manwel got into the van and started the engine. When it was his turn in the queue, he drove off the ferry. There were lots of boats, lots of people and a lot of noise.

Manwel drove through Mġarr and into the countryside. He arrived at a farm and pulled into the driveway, stopping the van near the house. He got out of the door and went towards the house, telling his wife, "I got some, I got some. Please, can you make me a nice rabbit stew, now?"

Hearing those words, Joe became scared. He did not want to be the main ingredient for dinner on Manwel's table. Then he noticed that Manwel had left the door of the van open. Joe slid onto the driver's seat and bounced out of the van, before sliding underneath it. He ran along beside the wall, where he spotted some bags of rubbish. He hid there to take a rest. Then he heard a small voice shout, "Get off my foot! GET OFF MY FOOT!" He looked down and saw a mouse. Moving his foot, Joe asked the mouse his name.

"I am Mario. Who are you?"

"My name is Joe Fenek and I am from Malta. I have been kidnapped by all these hunters with dogs and ferrets. They want to turn me into rabbit stew."

Mario smiled and said, "Seems like you have a problem there, Joe."

"Yes," said Joe. "Can you help me please?"

"I don't know," said Mario. "How do you want me to help you?"

Joe explained his need to get back to Malta, to his friends and family.

"Well," said Mario. "The only way I can think of, to help you, is to take you to my friend, Spikey."

"Who is Spikey, then?" asked Joe.

"Spikey is a hedgehog and my friend," said Mario. "He will know what to do and if he doesn't, he knows everyone around here and someone will know how to help."

Before they could go off to visit Spikey, Mario made sure that they could not be seen when they began running along the wall again.

He said to Joe, "Follow me."

Mario led the way across the fields until they came to the prickly pears, the weeds and the fig tree. There, among the leaves, was a piece of wood.

Mario knocked. The piece of wood moved and from under it came a small, prickly animal: Spikey.

Spikey looked and said, "What do you want, Mario?"

"I have a new friend here," said Mario. "His name is Joe. He's from Malta and has a bit of a problem. He needs to get back to Malta to see his family and friends, but he can't swim."

"Why does he need to swim?" laughed Spikey.

"Because," said Mario, "I see no other way for him to get back than to swim across the channel."

“There must be another way,” said Spikey, “but I need to think.” So he thought and he thought and he thought. Suddenly, his face lit up with a smile (in the way only hedgehogs can). “I know who might be able to help,” he said. “I’ll take Joe to see Horace.”

“Who is Horace?” asked Mario and Joe together.

“Horace is a horse. He lives in Għajnsielem.”

“So,” asked Mario, “how will Horace the horse be able to get Joe across the channel? He can’t swim all that way!”

“No, he can’t,” said Spikey, “but he might still be able to help. We need to take Joe to Horace and ask. Let me just leave Mrs Spikey a note to say where I am and we can go now.”

The three friends made their way across the fields to Horace’s stable. When they arrived, Spikey looked for the entrance, a hole in the stable door, and they slipped through in single file.

Spikey shouted out, “Horace, Horace.”

The horse turned his big head and spying Spikey, he said, "What are you doing here? You don't usually come here."

"Well," said Spikey, "I have come to ask if you can help my friend, Joe, here. He needs to get back to his friends and family in Malta."

"How can I help with that, then?" asked Horace.

"Well, I was thinking, Horace, that you could go to Malta to do your racing and there might be some way we could get Joe here across in your box when you go racing."

"Yes, we could. No problem there, Spikey. Unless you think my not going until tomorrow is a problem? So, Joe, you want to stay here with me for tonight until we can get you across to Malta tomorrow?"

"That would be wonderful, Horace, thank you. And I can go home to Mellieħa tomorrow?"

"Sure you can, my box goes right past there when I go racing. So the best thing is that for now, you get a comfy place here in the stable and get some rest. You are going to need your energy tomorrow."

After a good sleep, Horace woke Joe up and explained what would happen later.

“When my owner comes, he will lead me onto the horsebox. Once I am on and it’s safe for you, I will knock twice as a signal for you to run on.”

Joe agreed to this and they both waited for Horace’s trainer to arrive. Horace was led onto the box and while the stable boy was gathering all the equipment, Horace gave the two-knock signal to Joe.

The rabbit ran as fast as he could and hid at the front of the box.

Horace had told him to be as still as possible, not to be seen or heard.

The stable boy locked the rear of the horsebox and climbed into the passenger seat of the pick-up, beside the trainer. They set off for Mġarr and the journey to Malta. They boarded the ferry and the humans went on deck to get coffee.

Horace explained that they would need another signal in Mellieħa, for Joe to get safely off the horsebox and back to his family. So it was decided that Horace would make a lot of noise and fuss at the place that Joe needed to get out. This would make the stable boy or the trainer get out and open the box, to find out what was wrong.

At the top of the hill, close to the Red Tower, Horace made a lot of noise and banged with his feet. The trainer stopped the truck and came around to see what all the fuss was about. Opening the box, he tried to calm Horace with gentle words of comfort.

"Calm down, mate. We'll not be on the road for long, now." While this was happening, he did not see Joe leap out of the back of the box and run across the road into the field. He ran and ran to the Red Tower. He began

to look for the entrances to the burrow and could see that lots of damage had been done in some places.

Joe found a useable entrance and went in, calling for his friends and family. Then he heard a small murmur. He was suddenly surrounded by friends and family, all talking at once and wanting to know where he had been.

He recalled the tale of his adventure in Gozo, but his family and friends did not believe him. But children, we know that Joe really did go to Gozo, don't we? We went too.

Joe Fenek's good deed

It was a warm afternoon. Joe Fenek was planning to lie down in the sun near the Red Tower. Suddenly, Jimmy the rat came running up the hill.

Joe shouted, "Hi, Jimmy, what's up? Where are you going?"

"OH, MY WORD," shouted Jimmy. "Can you help me? My cousin, Tony, is stuck down a hole near where the humans are doing all those road works."

Joe and Jimmy went to look and see what was wrong. Down, in a deep hole, was Tony. He looked as though he had his tail stuck in some cement or ballast, or something.

"Are you alright there, Tony?" asked Joe.

"Not really," said Tony. "I have a problem with my tail; I am stuck. Can you help me get out?"

Joe looked at Tony and said, "Don't worry. We will get you out."

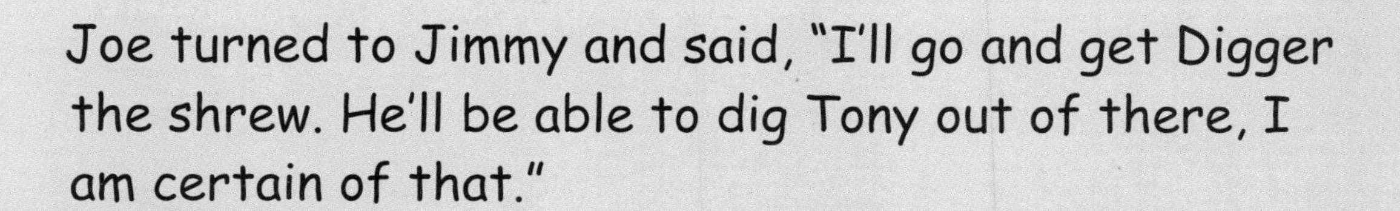

Joe turned to Jimmy and said, "I'll go and get Digger the shrew. He'll be able to dig Tony out of there, I am certain of that."

Leaving Jimmy to talk and keep Tony calm, Joe ran off towards Digger's home to ask for his help. As he

was running, he noticed a shadow on the ground. Stopping to quickly glance above him, Joe saw a sea-eagle diving towards him.

So he began to run and dodged between two, big stones into a hole. The sea-eagle swooped back into the sky, having missed a nice rabbit dinner.

Joe was just catching his breath when he heard a voice.

"Hello, Joe. What are you doing in my house?" It was Digger the shrew.

"Hello, Digger. I was on my way to your house, to ask for some help with a problem."

"What's wrong, Joe? You know I will help if I can."

Joe explained how Tony was stuck in a hole, near the road works that the humans were doing. Jimmy was there too, but not in the hole.

"We really need to go and help Tony get out of the hole. Please, will you came and help with the rescue, Digger?"

So Joe and Digger made their way back to the road works and the hole where Tony was stuck by the tail in the cement.

"Oh, my," said Digger. "It's far too deep to burrow and dig into there, to get to Tony safely."

"So how will we get him out, then?" asked Jimmy and Joe.

"I don't know, I don't know. I really don't know," said Digger, shaking his head.

Then Joe looked around and saw the long, plastic pipe lying on the ground nearby.

"Look," he said. "I wonder if we all worked together to move that pipe, if we could push it, so it goes into the hole? Then, when it's upright, you

could slide in and help Tony out? I will stay up here and make sure the pipe is safe."

Jimmy and Digger thought they could both get down the pipe to Tony, if Joe held the pipe steady. So the plan was decided upon.

"Look," said Jimmy. "The humans are coming." Having finished their lunch, the humans were putting their yellow safety vests back on and preparing to return to work.

"We need to be really quick," said Joe.

The three friends worked very quickly and the pipe was soon in the hole. While Joe steadied the pipe, Jimmy and Digger quickly slid down, to arrive where Tony was stuck by his tail in the cement.

They tried pulling Tony free, but it was not possible. Then Digger said, "Hang on, hang on! His tail is stuck in that cement." So Digger

clambered around to Tony's backside and pulled and pulled, and finally freed his tail. When Tony's tail was free, Jimmy pulled Tony's front paws and they were ready to run back up the pipe.

They scurried quickly as Joe was calling, "Be quick, be quick. They're here, they're here!"

Reaching the top of the pipe, the four friends, now together, ran onto the rough ground close by and looked for a place that was safe, so that they could stop and catch their breath.

When they looked down at the place where they had just been, the cement was being pumped into the hole and there were humans everywhere.

Joe turned to Tony and said, "You look like one, dirty rat."

They all laughed and made their way back to the tower where they could sit, rest and talk about their adventure.

Joe Fenek and the monster

Joe was excited. Today, his sister was going to visit him and she was bringing his two nephews, Andy and Brandon.

There was a voice calling, "Joe? Joe? Are you there?" Victoria and the boys had arrived. The boys ran towards him calling, "Hello, Uncle Joe."

Andy said, "Uncle Joe, mum has brought us some lunch: carrots and lettuce."

"Lovely," said Joe. "Just what I fancy."

Joe and his sister greeted each other as only rabbits knew how.

Then Victoria said, "Boys, why don't you go and play outside, while your uncle and I get the lunch sorted out."

So the boys went outside to play. After about 15 minutes, Brandon said, "Let's go down to the beach."

"OK," said Andy.

So they went down to the beach, making sure to take care when they crossed the busy road. So many cars and buses, a rabbit had to be careful that they remembered what their mum had told them.

They reached the beach and were playing on the rocks, when suddenly Andy shouted, "There's a monster, there's a monster!"

Coming out of the sea was a big, black monster.

It had one eye in the middle of its head; a big, orange hump on its back and HUGE, flat feet that looked like fish fins.

Both the small, boy rabbits were afraid and they hid behind a big rock. The monster came closer. The boys closed their eyes and held their breath. As the monster passed close to them, it sprayed water on them. They were shivering with fear.

After waiting for a few minutes, they looked to see if the monster was still there, but it had gone.

Brandon said to Andy, "We need to go and tell Uncle Joe about the monster and we need to go now."

So the boys ran back across the brush and the rocks to the road. They were careful to cross safely, even though they were both upset. They rushed back to Joe's burrow and ran indoors calling, "Uncle Joe, Uncle Joe. There's a monster, there's a monster!"

Joe went to meet the boys and said, "Whatever is going on? What do you mean, there's a monster?"

"There's a big, black monster at the beach, Uncle Joe. I think he is going to eat all the humans up."

"Where have you been? To the beach?" asked Victoria. "How many times must I tell you not to go running off. Those roads are too busy for small, boy rabbits to be playing near."

"We are sorry, Mum. We were just exploring and were very careful when we crossed the road. But we saw a monster - a big, black monster with one eye; a big, orange hump on his back and HUGE, black, flat feet."

Joe told Victoria he would take the boys back down to the beach and go and sort it all out. Meanwhile, Victoria would carry on getting lunch ready and they could all eat when he and the boys got back.

So Joe and the boys went to the beach, crossing the road very carefully. Joe looked carefully all across the beach, but he could not see any monsters. He saw humans, big and small, playing on the sand and swimming in the water.

After about 10 minutes of looking all around, Joe said to the boys, "I think this is all in your imagination. I can't see any monsters."

As they turned to leave and go back for lunch, Brandon suddenly shouted, "There's one, look! Coming out of the sea right now. A big, black monster with one eye."

Joe looked to where Brandon was pointing and he began to laugh.

"It's not funny, Uncle Joe. The monster is scary."

"Come with me, boys," said Joe, and he took the boys to hide behind some bigger rocks and watch the monster.

"Now," said Joe, "I want you to watch the monster."

So they watched as the monster came right out of the water and stopped. They were still afraid.

"He's taking his feet off, Uncle Joe, and his eye." Then the monster took off his big, orange hump.

The monster was not a monster at all. It was a human. Uncle Joe explained that humans sometimes dress themselves with masks, flippers and oxygen tanks, so that they could go and swim under the sea, to see the fish and other creatures that lived there.

"Come on," said Joe. "Let's go home and get some lunch, and you can tell Mum all about the scary monster that was really a diver."

Joe Fenek goes to the feast

It was a warm evening near the Red Tower and Joe was outside on the waste ground, enjoying the cooler part of the day, when along came Jimmy Rat.

"Hello, Jimmy, where are you going?" asked Joe.

"I'm off to the feast in Mellieħa village," replied Jimmy.

"You're going to the village? What sort of feast is there?" asked Joe.

"It's where all the humans go," said Jimmy. "They come and eat and dance, and they set fireworks off."

"So why are you going then?" asked Joe.

"I am going to get some free food, some very nice pizza, pies and sausage rolls."

"Where will you get that from, then?"

"Well, the humans are very untidy and drop all their leftovers on the ground. It just lies there. All I have to do is go and help myself. Why don't you come with me?" Jimmy asked.

"Oh, I don't know," said Joe. "It might be too noisy for me."

"No, it'll be fine. Come on."

So Joe followed Jimmy and off they went to the feast. They reached the back of the church

and Jimmy said, "I am STARVING, so I'm going to look for some food. Are you coming?"

"No, thanks," said Joe. "I'll stay here and just watch what is going on."

So Jimmy went off to get some food and Joe settled down to watch the humans. There were hundreds of them. They had long legs, short legs, boots, sandals and shoes. There were legs pushing wheels about and the wheels also had small humans on them. There were men singing, ladies singing, shouting and laughing – all very noisy for a rabbit's ears. There were bright lights and stalls selling all sorts of food and toys. The smells were lovely. It was mind boggling. Joe had never seen anything like it before. It was getting noisier and noisier. Then Jimmy came back.

"Joe, are you alright? What do you think of the feast then?"

"My word," said Joe. "I have never seen so many humans in one place all at once."

"It's good for us rats," said Jimmy.

"We can have a good old feed and there is plenty for all of us."

"Have you had your dinner then?" asked Joe.

"Yes, I have; thanks," said Jimmy. "I had some lovely pizza and some beer to drink."

"I think I have seen enough of the noisy feast," said Joe. "Can we go back now?"

"Oh, I would have liked to stay a little longer," said Jimmy. "But if you are tired and it's too noisy for you, then I'll walk back with you."

The two friends began to walk towards the road. Suddenly, Jimmy said, "Oh, my! It's a dog, it's a dog! Quick, let's get under that parked car."

The dog spotted them and came barking and growling, a bit too close for comfort.

"Come on, Joe. Run!" said Jimmy.

"I can't," said Joe. "My foot is stuck to the ground."

"What do you mean your foot is stuck? Stuck where? To what?"

"It's stuck to the ground in some pink, gooey stuff."

"Oh, no," said Jimmy, "here comes the dog!"

The dog was still barking and growling, and its teeth were all shiny and big. It was too big to get under the car, but Jimmy and Joe needed to get out so they could go home.

Jimmy went to look at where Joe's foot was stuck. Sure enough, there was pink, gooey stuff stuck between the road and Joe's foot. When Joe tried to move, the pink, gooey stuff stretched, but stayed stuck to both the road and Joe's foot.

The two friends were trying really hard to get Joe's foot out of the sticky mess. Suddenly there was a HUGE BANG, then another and another. Joe was terrified. "Oh, no!! The hunters are here, the hunters are here!" he screamed.

"No," said Jimmy. "Joe, it's the fireworks. It's just the fireworks."

Even the dog was upset. He was whimpering and squiggling out from under the car and around the legs of his human.

Joe was asking Jimmy to please free his foot from the pink, sticky goo. He wanted to move away from the noise and get home to the Red Tower where it was safe.

Jimmy and Joe worked together, and pulled and pulled and pulled. Suddenly, Joe's foot was free of the pink, stretchy goo and they could both run. They both started to run, but Joe's foot was a bit sticky, so he kept sticking to the road. Jimmy had an idea.

"Wait a minute, Joe. Stop, let me get a leaf." Jimmy took the leaf and wiped the sole of Joe's foot, and the sticky residue of the goo ended up on the leaf. Now the friends could run and run they did. They ran all the way back to the Red Tower.

Jimmy said, "I don't know. What a night! I am not taking you to the feast again."

"It wasn't my fault," said Joe. "If the humans put their rubbish in the bin, instead of dropping it on the ground and spitting chewing gum out, this sort of thing would not happen."

Jimmy was laughing. "I don't know. We'll have to call you 'Joe the stickyfoot rabbit.'"

They said goodnight and each of them went home to bed.

Joe Fenek and the chocolate

Joe was coming back from the village. He was walking across the waste ground when he saw Tony Rat walking towards him. He had all kinds of white stuff on his face and sugary stuff.

"Joe, Joe," said Tony. "Please help, Jimmy is caught in a mouse trap."

"What happened and where is he?" asked Joe.

"We were in the bakery," explained Tony, "eating all this nice, sugary stuff.

Tony stepped backwards and got his leg caught in the trap.

"OK," said Joe, "let's go and take a look." So Joe and Jimmy went down to the bakery.

"Right, then," said Joe. "How do we get in?"

"Through that hole there," said Tony, pointing to a hole in the wall.

"You are joking," said Joe. "I can't get through there."

Joe made his way around to the back of the building and found a plastic, curtain door which he could easily move with his nose. This led straight into the bakery. Jimmy followed this new route behind Joe.

They could see poor Tony there with his leg caught in the trap, right next to the leg of the big, metal table. Making their way towards him, they could see that Tony was in some pain.

Joe looked around while Jimmy was comforting his cousin. Joe noticed a metal spoon lying on the floor. So he went, picked it up and brought it back to where Tony was caught in the trap. He wedged the spoon handle in the trap, between the spring and the metal of the trap, and pushed his weight down.

The metal trap opened and Joe shouted, "Tony, pull Jimmy out NOW!"

Tony and Jimmy landed in a small heap. Meanwhile, Joe could not hold the spoon any longer and had to let go. It pinged up in the air and hit a metal bowl. The bowl tipped and from the top of the table poured all this brown, sticky liquid. The liquid landed on Jimmy and Joe.

Suddenly, there was a noise from the front of the bakery. A human shouted, "Is that you, Manwel? Manwel, is that you in there?"

The animals hid both under and behind the metal table, so that the human would not see them.

The human stood in the doorway. He looked in, spotted the bowl tipped over and saw the chocolate puddle. Again, he shouted, "Manwel! Fetch the mop! Deal with this chocolate spillage." The door swung closed.

Joe said, "Quick, Tony; help Tony onto my back. We need to get out of here."

Jimmy helped Tony to climb onto Joe's back, where the chocolate was all sticky. This helped Tony to stay on, even if it also spread onto Tony's fur.

The humans were coming back into the bakery room and there was a clatter of mops, buckets and doors.

"Come on, quickly. Follow me," said Joe.

The animals made their way back towards the plastic door they had come through on the way in, and didn't stop running until they got to the waste ground.

When Joe shouted, "Whoa," Jimmy and he stopped running.

"Let's get Tony off my back now," said Joe. "We need to see if he's alright."

Although Tony's foot was quite bruised, he was otherwise OK.

Joe wanted to know what the two rats had been doing in the bakery, in the first place.

"Listen," he told the rats. "You know you mustn't go where the humans are. You should not be eating all their stuff. Some of it is not good for our tummies."

"But it was so sweet and delicious," said Jimmy and Tony.

"I don't care how lovely and sweet it was. You should not have been in the bakery eating it. I want you to promise me that you will not go in the bakery ever again."

"We promise," said the rats.

Tony said, "Joe, you look like an Easter Bunny."

"Never mind the Easter Bunny," said Joe. "How am I going to get rid of all this chocolate on my fur?"

"Don't worry," said Tony. "When we get home, we can pick it off. Then we can eat all that lovely chocolate."

The Rabbit and the ghost

Jimmy and Tony were on the way home from a night out in Mellieħa and were nearly home, near the Red Tower, when they saw a white figure.

Jimmy said to Tony, "It looks like a ghost."

They ran and hid behind the rocks, and took a sneak peek. They looked and saw a white, ghostly-looking rabbit.

Tony turned to Jimmy and said, "I think you are right, it's a ghost. What are we going to do?"

"Don't worry," said Jimmy. "We will just stay here and watch and wait until it goes away."

So the two rats stayed and watched. Then the ghost disappeared, so they went home and had a good rest.

The next morning, the two rats went to see Joe Fenek at his burrow. Joe was just coming out of the entrance to see what the weather was doing.

"Hello, Joe," chorused Tony and Jimmy.

"Hello, you two," said Joe. "What are you doing this way?"

"Coming to see you," said Tony.

"What do you need to see me about?" asked Joe.

The rats explained, "Last night on the way home from Mellieħa, we saw a ghost. The ghost of a rabbit."

"A ghost?" said Joe, "the ghost of a rabbit? There is no such thing as a ghost."

"Yes, there is," Jimmy said, "because we saw it, didn't we, Tony?"

"Yes, we did. Really, we did, Joe."

Jimmy asked Joe to join them the same night, to see if they could spot the same ghost.

"OK," said Joe. "I'll meet up with you, but there is no such thing as a ghost."

At six o'clock that evening, the two rats met up with Joe and made their way across the waste land towards the Red Tower. They found the rock where they had hidden the previous night and they watched and waited. An hour went by, then another.

Jimmy suddenly whispered, "There it is. There's the ghost, just near the tower!"

Joe and Tony looked to where Jimmy was pointing and saw what he meant.

"I am not sure it's a ghost, Jimmy, but I can see what you mean. I am going to go around the tower and get behind whatever it is, to have a better look."

"Right, Joe," said Jimmy, "but be careful."

Joe made his way to the other side of the tower and was looking to see the ghostly figure. Suddenly, there was a white face before him: a white face with a pair of pink eyes.
Joe was a bit scared, but thought that he needed to say something.

So he said,
"Are you a ghost?"

"A ghost?" said the white face with pink eyes. "No, I am not a ghost."

"Can I touch you?" asked Joe.

"Yes," said the white figure.

Joe reached out and said to the figure, "No, you are not a ghost, but who are you and what are you doing up here?"

"My name is Harvey and I am a tame rabbit. I don't usually live out in the wild like you seem to," said the visitor. "I live in a nice, clean hutch. I got out of the open door of my hutch and came exploring. Trouble is, I can't find my way back to the hutch. I think I am lost."

"Oh," said Joe. "One of those posh rabbits, living in a hutch. Do you know where you live? Where your hutch is?"

"It's in the pet shop, in the village," said Harvey. "But I don't know my way back and I am lost and hungry."

"Follow me," said Joe. He took Harvey down to meet the rats.

Joe explained that Harvey was not a ghost, but a New Zealand, white rabbit who needed to get back to the village pet shop. Jimmy explained to Harvey that he would not be able to get back into the pet shop right now, as it was dark and the shop was closed, and all the doors were locked.

Harvey asked Jimmy, "So can I come to your place tonight and you can look after me, and take me home in the morning?"

"Sorry, but no," said Jimmy. "We can't look after rabbits in our place. You will have to stay for the night in Joe's burrow and we'll take you home in the morning."

The next morning, the rats arrived at Joe's place to collect Harvey and take him home. The four friends went to the village and located the pet shop. They looked all around the shop for a way in and found

a hole in the fence. Sadly, the hole was too small for Harvey to get through.

Joe said, “So how will we get Harvey back into his nice, warm hutch?”

“I know how,” said Jimmy. “Come with me.”

The four animals made their way to the front of the shop, where Jimmy told Harvey to wait outside the front door until he was called. Joe pushed the shop door with his nose and the door opened. Jimmy ran in and there was a human lady buying pet food. Tony and Jimmy knew that humans were frightened of rats like them and were not surprised when the lady screamed and dropped the pet food she was carrying, all over the floor.

The humans were not really concentrating on the animals and Jimmy called Harvey to come into the shop.

Once in, Jimmy said to Harvey, "There, now you are home. Go and find your bed and have a nice sleep."

"Thanks, so much," said Harvey.

Meanwhile, the rats and Joe were running out of the shop and away up the street. They stopped, turned and looked back, just in time to see the pet shop owner scoop Harvey up from the floor and return him to his hutch.

Joe said to the two rats, "That's another good job; a good deed done."

The rats chorused, "Yes, it is. And now it's time to go home and have lunch."

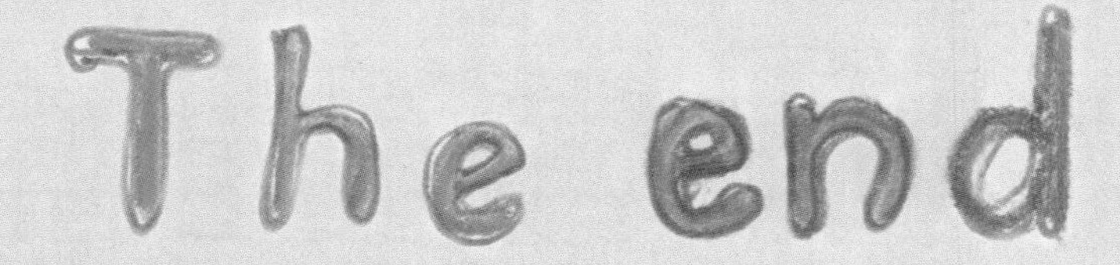

Make a photocopy of the above scene taken from page 10 and COLOUR it using your own creativity.

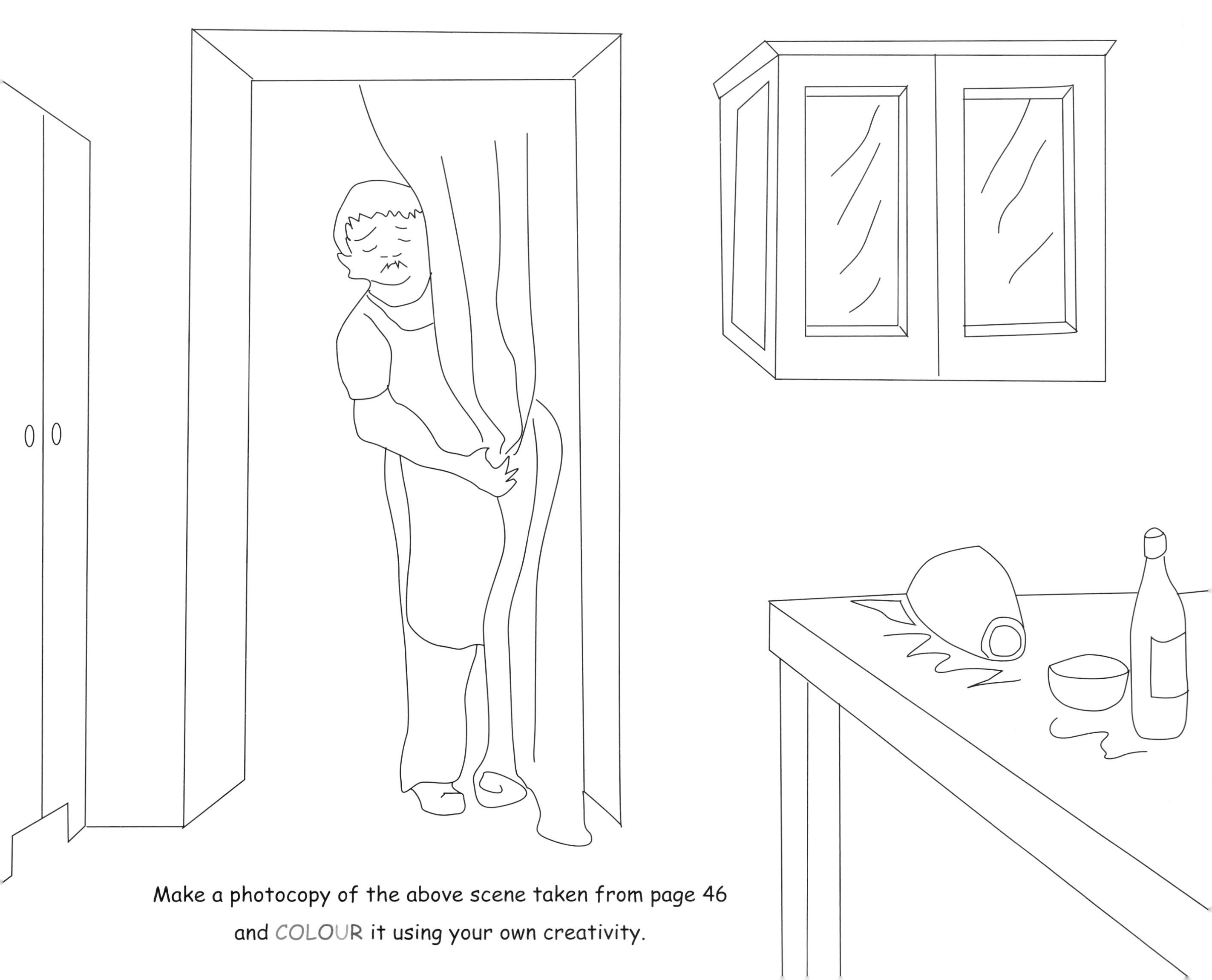

Make a photocopy of the above scene taken from page 46 and COLOUR it using your own creativity.

Other Books published by

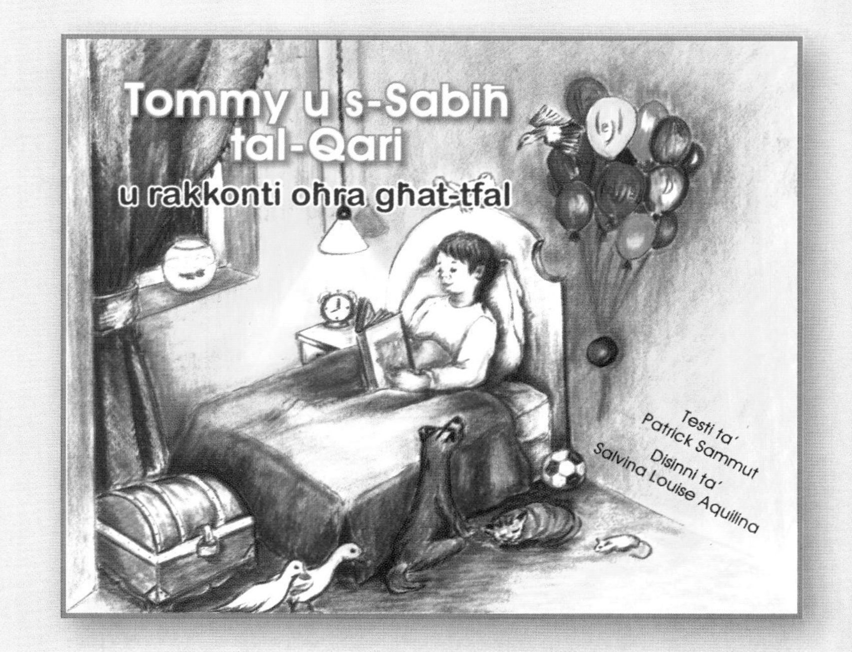